HAVE YOU HEARD ABOUT EPIC! YET?

We're the largest digital library for kids, used by millions in homes and schools around the world. We love stories so much that we're now creating our own!

With the help of some of the best writers and illustrators in the world, we create the wildest adventures we can think of. Like a mermaid and narwhal who solve mysteries. Or a pet made out of slime.

We hope you have as much fun reading our books as we had making them!

Kitty AND DRAGON

MEIKA HASHIMOTO
ILLUSTRATED BY GILLIAN REID

Andrews McMeel
PUBLISHING®

PART ONE

Kitty lives in a barn.

It is a very noisy barn.

WHINNY

MOO

BAA

The horses whinny.

The cows moo.

The sheep baa.

The pigs oink.

The chickens SQUAWK!

OINK

SQUAWK.

Kitty does not like noise.

Kitty leaves the very noisy barn.

She will look for a new home.

A quiet home.

Kitty goes into town.
She passes
the spell and potion shop.
She passes the milk shop
and the tea shop.

The shops are too noisy.

Kitty keeps walking.

Kitty enters a forest.
At first, it is very quiet.

Fairies fly over to Kitty.

"Beware the silent dragon!"
they shout.

"Beware his fiery breath!"

The fairies are very noisy.

Kitty keeps walking.

Kitty comes to a swamp.

A frog jumps out of the water.

"Beware the silent dragon!"

he croaks.

More frogs jump
out of the water.

"Beware the silent dragon!"
they croak.

"Beware his long, sharp claws!"
Frog voices fill the swamp.

Kitty is not scared.
She keeps walking.

Kitty reaches a valley
with green, grassy hills.
Suddenly,
the ground begins to shake.

The hills are full
of stomping giants.

"Beware the silent
dragon!" they yell.

"Beware his spiky tail!"

Kitty sighs.

She keeps walking.

Kitty arrives at
a mountain.
It is very tall.
She starts to climb.

And climb.

Kitty climbs above the noisy barn.

She climbs above the noisy town.

She climbs above the noisy forest,

the noisy swamp,

and the noisy hills.

On top of the mountain,

Kitty finds a cave.

She goes inside.

It is very quiet inside the cave.

There is a warm fire.
There is a soft rug.

Kitty is tired.

She curls up on the rug.

She takes a nap.

When Kitty wakes up,

she sees a dragon.

He has fiery breath.

He has long, sharp claws.

He has a spiky tail.

But Kitty is not afraid.
"Hello, Dragon,"
Kitty says.
"I am looking for
a new home.
A quiet home.
Can I stay here
with you?"

Dragon smiles.

He wags his tail.

He nods.

He is so happy
to have
a new friend!

Dragon makes Kitty her very own rug.

He brings her fresh milk.

Kitty trims
Dragon's claws.

She chases
the mice away.

Dragon likes

living with Kitty.

Kitty likes
living with Dragon.

At night, Dragon tucks Kitty
under his wing.
Together, the two friends fall asleep.

Kitty is happy
in her new, quiet home.

PART TWO

KITTY GETS A COLD

One morning,
Dragon goes outside.

The sky is blue.
The wind is blowing.

It is the perfect day
to fly a kite.

Dragon finds his kite.

He waits for Kitty to wake up.

When Kitty opens her eyes,
she groans.
"My nose is stuffy," she tells Dragon.
"My throat hurts.
My head—ah…Ah…AH…

CHOO!"

"I have a cold," Kitty says.
"I cannot fly a kite.
I need to be alone
so I can rest."

Kitty closes her eyes.
She falls asleep.

Dragon tries to fly his kite
all by himself.
But it is no fun
without Kitty.

Dragon has an idea.

He will help Kitty get better.

He goes to his library.

He reads books
about taking care of
kitties who have colds.

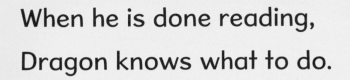

When he is done reading,
Dragon knows what to do.

Caring
for
Kitties
with
Colds

Dragon goes to the kitchen.

He boils water.

He pours it into a big cup.

He adds a tea bag.

He stirs in honey.

Dragon puts a cup of hot tea
next to Kitty.

Kitty drinks the tea.

It soothes her sore throat.

She goes back to sleep.

Dragon makes soup for Kitty.

He chops onions, garlic,

carrots, and celery.

He cooks them
in a pot.
He adds broth.

Dragon stirs in fish and herbs.

Finally, he adds some noodles.

He simmers the soup
until the noodles are done.

Dragon ladles the soup into a bowl.

Dragon puts
the bowl of soup
next to Kitty.

Kitty eats the soup.

It warms her tummy.

She goes back to sleep.

Dragon looks for sewing supplies.
He digs for a bag of fabric.

Dragon watches his crystal ball
to learn how to quilt.

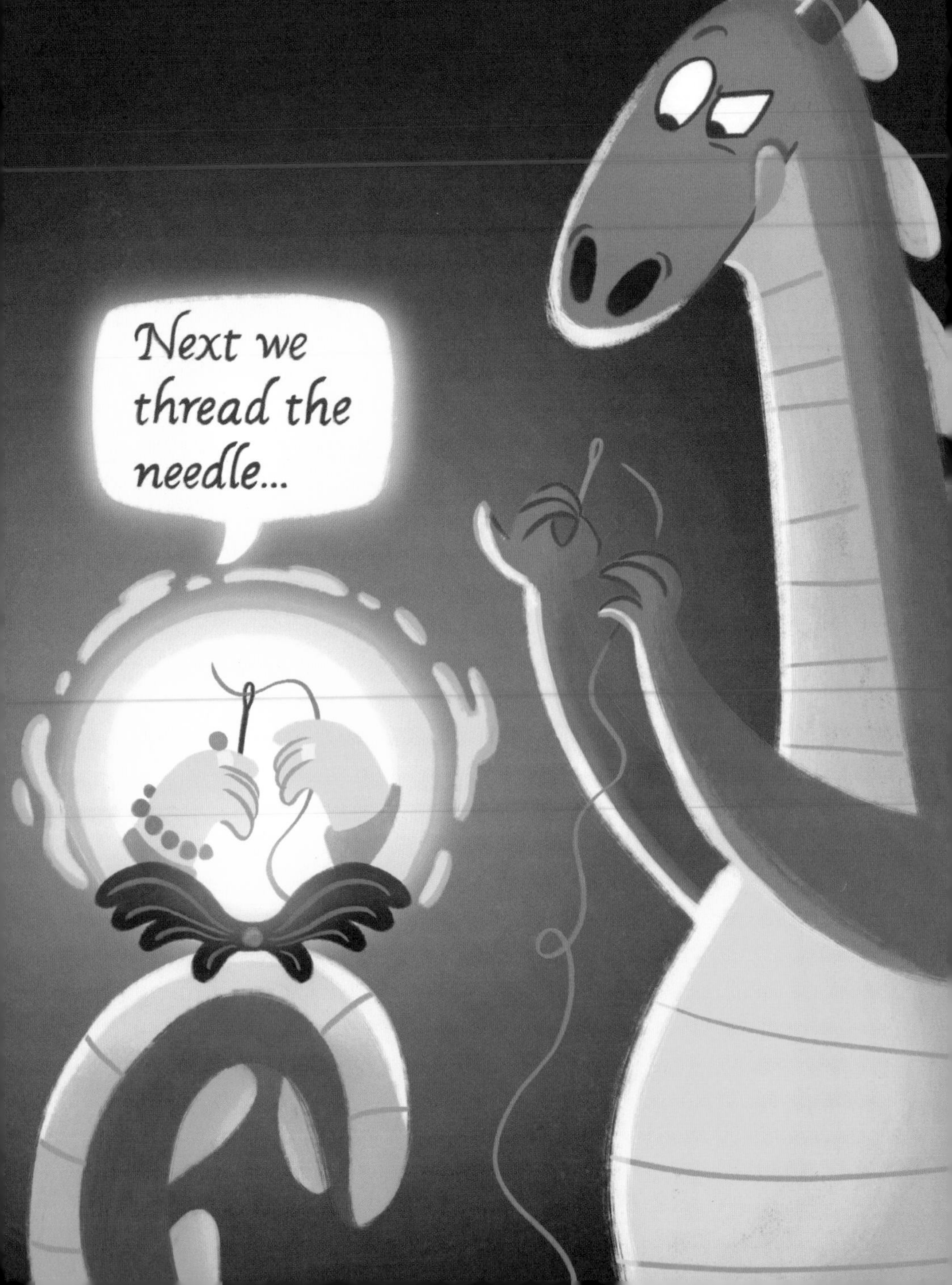

Dragon begins to sew
for the first time.

Dragon is not happy with his first try.

It does not look
quite right.
He pulls out the
thread.

He starts again.

When he is done,

Dragon has a blanket.

It looks a little strange.

But it is very warm.

Dragon puts the blanket over Kitty.
He is careful not to wake her.

Kitty sleeps all night.

In the morning, Kitty wakes up.
She stretches her legs.
She clears her throat.

"I feel better!" she says.
"Thank you for the hot tea.
Thank you for the
fish noodle soup.
Thank you for the warm
blanket!"

Dragon smiles.

He gives Kitty the kite.

Together,
Dragon and Kitty
fly the kite
in the sunny, windy sky.

Ah...Ah...AH...
CHOO!
CARING for DRAGONS WITH COLDS
CARING FOR DRAGONS WITH COLDS

PART THREE

Kitty AND DRAGON

KITTY TIDIES UP

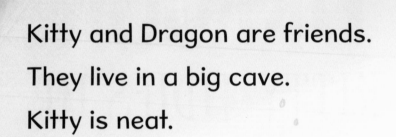

Kitty and Dragon are friends.

They live in a big cave.

Kitty is neat.

Dragon is messy.

Kitty washes her dishes.
Dragon leaves his dishes
on the table.

Kitty sweeps up.
Dragon tracks dirt
all over the floor.

Kitty brushes her teeth carefully.
Dragon gets toothpaste
all over the
mirror.

Kitty is tired
of tidying up by herself.
She has an idea.
She leaves the cave
and goes down
the mountain.

She walks
over the hills,
past the swamp,
and through the forest.
She reaches
the potion shop.

Kitty goes into the shop.
A wizard greets her.

Kitty asks the wizard
for a potion to make
Dragon tidier.

The wizard rolls up his sleeves.
He takes out a big pot.

He adds
a dishcloth to the pot.
He adds
a broom, a dustpan,
soap, and water.

He chants
a magic spell.

The wizard pours
the potion into a bottle.
"Sprinkle three drops
of this tidying-up potion
onto Dragon every day,"
he says.

Kitty sprinkles
three drops of the potion
onto Dragon.

Suddenly,
Dragon SEES
the dirty dishes.

He SEES
the dirt
on the floor.

He SEES
the toothpaste
on the mirror.

He SEES
the awful mess!

Dragon washes the dishes
until they sparkle.

He sweeps the floor
again and again.

Dragon polishes
the bathroom mirror.
He scrubs the tub.
He wipes the sink.
Kitty is happy.
The cave is very clean.

But then,
Dragon grabs Kitty's dishes
before she finishes her lunch.

Dragon sweeps all day.

He is too busy sweeping to play with Kitty.

At bedtime,

Kitty brushes her teeth.

Dragon cleans the mirror

over and over again.

That night,
Kitty cannot sleep.

She misses the old Dragon.

Kitty gets up.

She goes to the sink.

She pours out the potion.

The next morning,
the potion
has worn off.
Dragon is messy again.

Kitty gets another idea.

"Dragon," says Kitty,
"while I do the dishes,
will you dry them?"

Kitty sweeps the floor.

"Dragon," says Kitty,
"will you hold
the dustpan for me?"

"Dragon," says Kitty,
"if I clean the sink
and the tub,
will you wipe
the mirror?"

Kitty and Dragon
clean the cave together.
It is quick.
It is fun!

When they are done,
they still have time
to play.

Kitty is glad
that the cave is clean
and Dragon is back
to his old self.

PURRRR

MEIKA HASHIMOTO grew up on a shiitake mushroom farm in Maine. She is a children's book editor and lives deep in the woods with her husband, two rescue mutts, and a calico cat. She is the author of *The Magic Cake Shop*, *The Trail*, and *Scaredy Monster*.

GILLIAN REID is an illustrator from the United Kingdom who now lives in Canada. She has a degree in animation production and also works as a character designer for children's television. She loves to listen to history podcasts while she draws.

Andrews McMeel Publishing
a division of Andrews McMeel Universal
1130 Walnut Street, Kansas City, Missouri 64106

www.andrewsmcmeel.com

Epic! Creations, Inc.
702 Marshall Street, Suite 280,
Redwood City, California 94063

www.getepic.com

20 21 22 23 24 SDB 10 9 8 7 6 5 4 3 2 1

ISBN: 978-1-5248-6100-1

Library of Congress Control Number: 2020935430

Design by Wendy Gable and Dan Nordskog

Made by:
King Yip (Dongguan) Printing & Packaging Factory Ltd.
Address and location of manufacturer:
Daning Administrative District, Humen Town
Dongguan Guangdong, China 523930
1st Printing—7/13/20

LOOK FOR THESE GREAT BOOKS FROM

epic!